"Practice makes perfect!" It is through practice that children gain self-confidence and proficiency in their reading and writing skills. And parents can help. The stories and activities in **Hello Reader! Hello Writer!** books enable a parent to support and enhance the reading and writing strategies that are taught in school.

The stories in **Hello Reader! Hello Writer!** books are written with familiar words and short sentences that emerging readers can handle. Games and activities provide practice with skills such as word building, sentence building, grammar, reading comprehension, listening comprehension, following directions, and handwriting and letter formation. Best of all, the stories are fun to read, and the activities are fun to do!

So enjoy the story! Enjoy the activities! And most of all, enjoy your new reader!

Strategies for Sounding Out New Words
If your child comes to a word he or she doesn't know, encourage him or her to try one of these techniques:
• Say the beginning sound.
• Try the vowel sound. (Skip the vowel if it's too hard.)
• Say the ending sound.
• Blend the sounds together.
• Think of another word that looks like this word or rhymes with it.
• Look for familiar word parts or syllables.
• Talk to your brain: What word fits in the sentence? What makes sense?
• Look for picture clues.

About the Activities
The activities in this book are designed to enhance and accelerate learning. They are not meant to be done in one sitting. You should take your cues from your child. Some children enjoy paper and pencil tasks and written reinforcement. Other children try to avoid any written tasks.

You can encourage, reinforce, and prompt. But time spent together should be fun and stress-free. If your child becomes tired, put the book away for another time.

On most pages, you will need to read the instructions to your child.

To Jill
— G.M.

For Mom
— L.F.

ISBN 0-439-33016-5

Text copyright © 2001 by Grace Maccarone.
Literacy Activities copyright © 2001 by Alayne Pick.
Illustrations copyright © 2001 by Laura Freeman.
All rights reserved. Published by Scholastic Inc.
SCHOLASTIC, HELLO READER, CARTWHEEL BOOKS, and associated logos are trademarks and/or registered trademarks of Scholastic Inc.

10 9 8 7 6 5 4   03 04 05

Printed in the U.S.A.
First printing, October 2001

I See a Leaf

Story by Grace Maccarone
Literacy Activities by Alayne Pick
Illustrated by Laura Freeman

Hello Reader! Hello Writer!
Level 1

SCHOLASTIC INC.
New York   Toronto   London   Auckland   Sydney
Mexico City   New Delhi   Hong Kong

Kate and Jill are walking to school.

"I see a leaf," says Jill.

"I will give it to Miss Hill."

"I see a leaf," says Kate.

"I will give it to Miss Hill."

Kate and Jill see Jack.
"I have a red leaf
for Miss Hill," says Kate.
"Jill has a yellow leaf
for Miss Hill."

"So?" says Jack. "I will give her two leaves…

four leaves…

more and more leaves!"

Jill, Kate, and Jack
carry the leaves to class.
They see Miss Hill.

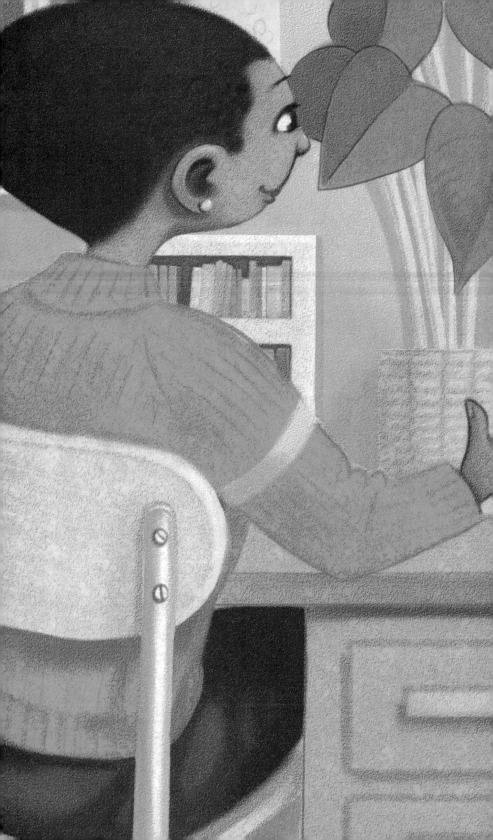

"This red leaf is for you,"
says Kate.
"This yellow leaf is for you,"
says Jill.

"These are for you,"
says Jack.
Miss Hill is surprised.

"Thank you,"
says Miss Hill.
"Let's make a tree."

And they do.

WORD LIST

a	I	says
all	is	school
and	it	see
are		so
	Jack	surprised
carry	Jill	
class		thank
	Kate	these
do		they
	leaf	this
for	leaves	to
four	let's	tree
		two
give	make	
	Miss	walking
has	more	will
have		
her	red	yellow
Hill		you

Make-a-Word

- Cut out the letters **n**, **w**, **k**, **l**, **a**, **i**, and **g**.
- Starting at the green dot, put the word **an** in the word tray.
- Change one letter to make **in**.
- Add one letter to make the ending **ing**.
- Add one letter to make **wing**. (You will have to shift three letters to the right.)
- Change one letter to make **king**. Take **king** off your word tray, but keep the letters together.
- Look at the remaining three letters. Make the word part **wal**, and put it in your word tray. Listen to the vowel in the middle. Listen to the beginning and ending sounds.
- Add **king** to the word part **wal**. Think about what the word sounds like now: **walking**. Say the word parts together smoothly.
- Study the word with your eyes. Now scramble the letters.

- Respell the word with the letters.
- Scramble the letters and spell again.
  If spelling the word from memory is too
  hard, look at the word as it is spelled out
  on page 18, and match the letters.
- Write the word from memory.

n w k l a i g

WORD TRAY

Skill: Word Building

Punctuation Pointers

"I see a leaf," says Kate.

Read this sentence.

Point out all the punctuation.

Quotation marks show what a person is saying.

With your left pointer finger, point to the beginning quotation mark (near the word **I**). With your right pointer finger, point to the end quotation mark (after the word **leaf**). Read what Kate is saying aloud. Read the words between your fingers—the words between the quotation marks.

Point to the comma.
A comma tells you to take a breath and stop for a short time before you begin to read again. Read the sentence. Take a breath after the word **leaf**.

Point to the period.
A period is a stop at the end of a sentence. Read the whole sentence. Stop when you get to the period.

Skill: Punctuation

Sentence Cut-Ups

Use scissors to cut apart the sentence
in the pink box.
Leave all punctuation attached to the
closest word.

Scramble the words.
Unscramble the words to remake
the sentence.
Use punctuation as clues:

   " " show what Kate says

   , tells you to take a breath

   . shows the end of the sentence

CAPITAL LETTERS show the beginning of
a sentence, the word **I**, or a name.

Play it again!

"I | see | a | leaf," | says | Kate.

I see a leaf," says Kate.

Make it harder!

Cut apart the sentence in the blue box.

Remake the sentence.

Put the quotation marks, comma, and
period where they belong.

Play it again!

Word Leaves

Look back at the
story to find words
that fit in each leaf

Words that tell names:
_____
_____
_____
_____
_____

Words that tell colors:
_____
_____
_____

Words that tell how much:
_____
_____
_____
_____

Words that show actions (what you can do):

____

____

____

____

____

Words that are things:

____

____

____

____

____

ANSWERS: Words that tell names: Jill, Kate, Jack, Miss Hill; Words that tell colors: yellow, red; Words that tell how much: a, two, four, more; Words that show actions: walking, see, give, carry; Words that are things: school, leaf, class, tree

Skill: Grammar

Sound Boxes

Write the word you just heard.

Write the word you just heard.
The silent **a** is already there for you.

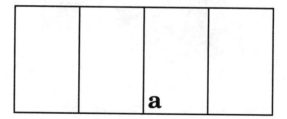

Write the word you just heard.
The broken line means that you can
write the same letter in the next box.

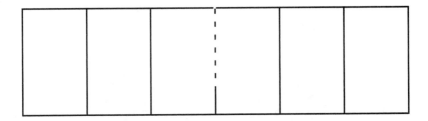

Happy Handwriting

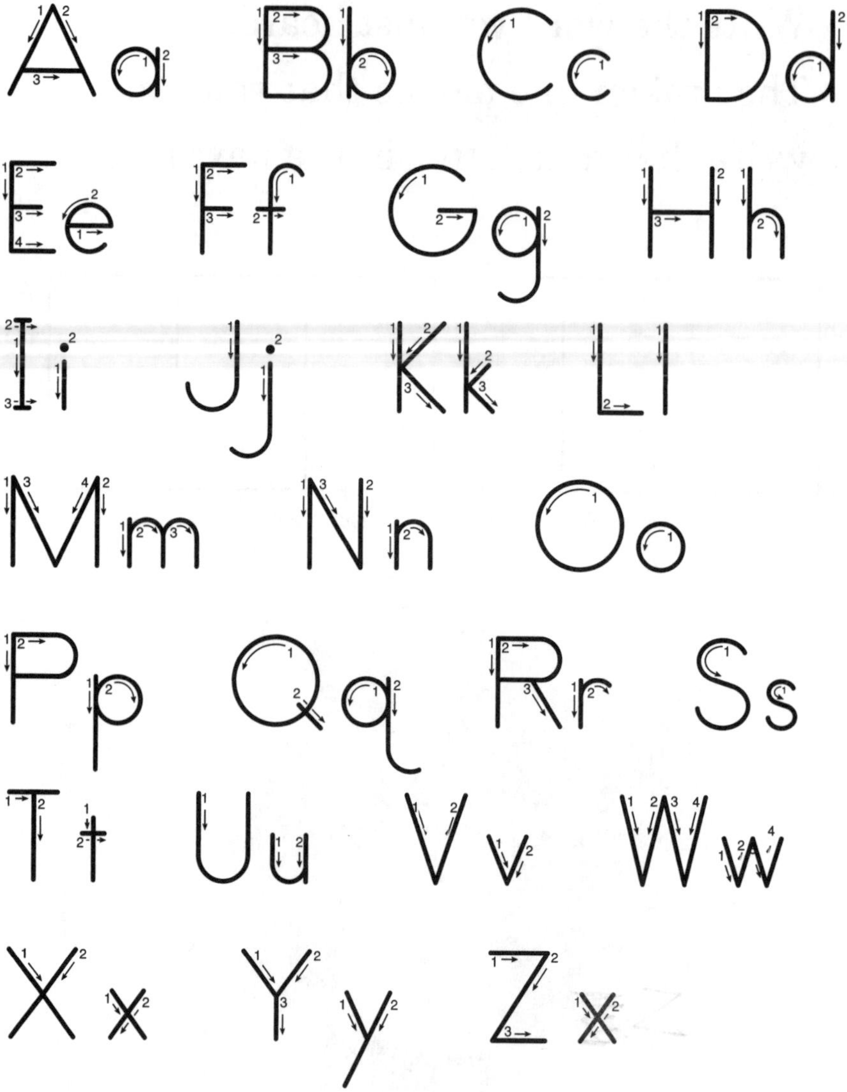

Aa Bb Cc Dd

Ee Ff Gg Hh

Ii Jj Kk Ll

Mm Nn Oo

Pp Qq Rr Ss

Tt Uu Vv Ww

Xx Yy Zx

Use the chart above to help you copy the
sentence at the top of the next page. Leave
a space as wide as your finger between
each word.

has

YOUR NAME

a yellow leaf.

To the parent: Have your child use a thick pencil. Grippers that are placed over regular pencils can be very helpful to new writers.

As your child copies the sentence, pay close attention to his or her letter formation. All circles should be formed from the top down— not from the bottom up. To cue your child to the proper circle letter formation, have him or her hold his or her left hand in a semi-circle. The forefinger is the correct starting place; the pencil moves counter-clockwise.

Skill: Letter Formation

Really Writing

Use the words **red, leaf,** and **yellow** in a sentence.

Remember:
- Begin the sentence with a capital letter.
- Use a finger space between each word.
- End the sentence with the period.

_____

_____

_____

_____

_____

Draw a picture to go with your sentence.

Skill: Sentence Writing

Which Way Did They Go?

Help Kate, Jill, and Jack take their leaves to school for Miss Hill. Follow the path from each child to Miss Hill's desk.